Monkey in the Stars

If you enjoy reading this book, you might also like to try another story from the **MAMMOTH STORYBOOK** series:

Monkey
in the Stars

Jamila Gavin

illustrated by
Anthony Lewis

Mammoth

For Miriam
who kept on asking for
a Diwali story

J.G.

First published in Great Britain 1998
by Mammoth, an imprint of Egmont Children's Books Limited
Michelin House, 81 Fulham Road, London SW3 6RB

Text copyright © 1998 Jamila Gavin
Illustrations copyright © 1998 Anthony Lewis

The rights of Jamila Gavin and Anthony Lewis to be identified as
the author and illustrator of this work have been asserted by them
in accordance with the Copyright, Designs and Patents Act 1988

ISBN 0 7497 2914 7

10 9 8 7 6 5 4 3 2 1

A CIP catalogue record for this book
is available from the British Library

Printed in Great Britain by Cox & Wyman Ltd,
Reading, Berkshire

Contents

~

1 Monkey on the wardrobe

'Ow!' Amrita sat bolt upright, fully awake. Moonlight flooded into her room through the open window. There was a strange silence, broken from time to time by something cracking and crunching. She looked around trying to work out what the sound was and where it was coming from. Something hard and small rolled into her hand. She fingered it curiously, trying to identify it in the dark- ness. It was the size of a large pea pod, but ridged

1

and brittle. She squeezed it and it cracked loudly.

A strange high voice piped from nowhere, 'That's an empty shell. Here have this.' A small object flew through the air and struck her on the nose.

'Ow!' Amrita switched on the light. 'Ow, ow, ow!' she squealed, as she was pelted by another and another. And then she saw the mess. Scattered on the sheets and all over the carpet were . . . monkey-nuts! 'Oh my goodness! What a mess!'

'Go on, open it, eat it, eat it! These peanuts are excellent,' came the voice again – a voice which hardly seemed human. It was crackly, chattery, ripply, giggly – and, as it spoke, a shower of empty peanut shells cascaded down from the top of the wardrobe.

'Hey!' protested Amrita, raising her arms to protect herself.

At first, all Amrita could see was a long, coiling, hairy, silver tail. Then, from within the depths of the shadows at the top of the wardrobe, she made out a curved body shining with silver fur, a round, black, leathery face, two mischievous eyes glinting from beneath furry eyebrows and a grinning mouth, inside which she could see a row of sharp, white, star-bright teeth.

'Here, have another!' A monkey-nut hurtled down. Amrita automatically caught it. 'Good catch!' trilled the creature.

'What are you?' Amrita finally gasped.

The creature leapt from the wardrobe, swung from the ceiling light and landed with a plop on her bed. 'What do you mean, what am I? Can't you see?' He wagged a black, bony, long-nailed finger at her. 'What's this?' He stroked his long fur. 'What's this?' He bounded on all four legs round the room. 'What's this?' He stood upright on two legs, getting taller and taller and taller till his ears brushed the ceiling. 'And what's this?' He looped up his great serpentine tail, which

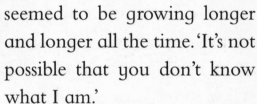

seemed to be growing longer and longer all the time. 'It's not possible that you don't know what I am.'

'You look like a monkey, but . . .' stammered Amrita, sliding down under the sheets, till only her eyes and the tip of her nose showed above the covers.

'Look like a monkey, indeed, but . . . but what?' snorted the creature.

'You're not any old monkey!' she finished weakly.

'How observant of you,' he scoffed. 'Of course I'm not just any old monkey.' He leapt from her bed and landed on the window ledge. Outlined in the moonlight, he looked silver and gold, animal and human, tiny but gigantic, light and shade . . . he looked like . . .

'Hanuman!' Amrita whispered the name.

'Ah-ha!' the monkey breathed with satisfaction, and a light wind rippled all round the room, ruffling Amrita's hair, billowing the curtains and scattering the monkey-nut shells across the floor. 'Yessss!' he proclaimed, his voice suddenly sounding like distant rain.

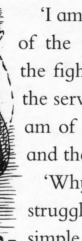

'I am Hanuman, Lord of the Monkeys. I am the fighter against evil, the servant of Vishnu. I am of the past, present and the future.'

'Why . . .?' Amrita struggled to form the simple question.

'Why am I here?' Hanuman asked it for her. 'Why am I here? Why am I there? Why am I anywhere?' he answered teasingly. He flicked his tail across the room. It fell in a blaze of sparks across her bed. 'Hold on to my tail, little Amrita. Come with me!

Diwali, the Festival of
Light, begins tomorrow.
All over the world,
the tailors have been
at work, cutting and
sewing new garments
from woven cloth, and
the dye-workers have
cast the cloth into
wonderful colours. Let's see
if the walls of every home have been
whitewashed and the floors swept clean
and decorated to welcome the Goddess
Lakshmi. Let's see if evil has been driven
from the universe. Let's see if Prince
Rama has defeated the King of the
Demons and rescued Princess Sita.'

Amrita jumped out of bed. 'Oh yes,
let's!' She clasped the Monkey God's tail.
She wound it round her like a sash. 'I'm
ready!' she cried, flinging wide her

window. With one bound, Hanuman leapt among the stars with Amrita safely entwined in his tail.

2 Tricked by the demon

Princess Sita huddled into the old trunk of a banyan tree, whose twisting creepers hung like a cage around her. The demons danced and shrieked, circling her like a band of moths round a flame. Every now and then they thrust their long claw-like fingers through the leaves to pinch and poke at her.

'Oh, Rama, Rama!' she wept. 'Will I ever see you again? It's all my fault. Lakshmana was right – it was a trick.'

Sita lived in the jungle with her exiled husband, Prince Rama. His father wanted him to rule the Kingdom of Ayodhya, but his second queen wanted her son, Prince Bharata, to be king. Years ago, she had saved the king's life and, in return, he had granted her two wishes. For a long time she did not use the wishes, but now she demanded that Bharata be crowned king and that Rama should be banished to the jungle for fourteen years.

Everyone knew this was like a death sentence, for the jungle was full of wild animals and demons, and they were

horrified when Sita said she would go with her husband. Prince Lakshmana, Rama's younger brother, asked for permission to go with them and, with a breaking heart, the old king agreed. So the three left the kingdom.

They had been in the forest for some time when Sita saw the most beautiful creature in the world — a deer, whose golden fur had patterns like shining moons and whose horns were twisted with silver and tipped with sapphires and diamonds. She longed to have its fur for a cloak. When she told Rama about it, he immediately grasped his bow and unsheathed his arrows, ready to hunt the deer.

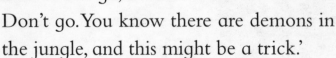

Lakshmana warned him: 'Don't go, brother! Don't go. You know there are demons in the jungle, and this might be a trick.'

But Rama said, 'Look at Sita. She is a princess, yet she looks like a beggar. She has given up everything by joining me here and, until now, she has never asked me for anything. How can I refuse her this one request? I'm sure I will be all right, but promise me, Lakshmana, protect my Sita while I am away. Do not leave her alone – not for one minute.'

Lakshmana promised, and Rama sped away, his bow and arrow at the ready. But Rama didn't come back. Then, from out of the jungle came a cry which sent the parrots hurtling into the air. 'Lakshmana, Lakshmana! Oh, brother, help me! My life is in danger! Come and save me! Quick, before it's too late!'

Lakshmana and Sita clasped each other in terror. Then Lakshmana grabbed his spear, and he was about to rush into the jungle to save his brother when he remembered his pledge never to leave Sita alone. He stopped and fell to his knees.

Sita was bewildered, then angry. 'Lakshmana, why do you hesitate? Are you afraid? Are you such a coward that you don't go this instant to save my husband?'

Lakshmana was in tears. 'How can I, Sita? I promised Rama I would not leave you alone for one single moment. How can I disobey him?'

Sita's anger was terrible. 'If you don't go and save my husband, I will never call you brother again. If you don't go, I will!'

Rama's terrified voice continued to plead. 'Help me, help me! Come quickly! Save me!'

Lakshmana took a piece of chalk and drew a circle all round the hut, chanting special prayers as he did so. 'Sita, I will go and search for Rama but, whatever you do, do not step outside this circle. It will protect you from all evil.' Then he left her all alone.

Hours went by, and neither Rama nor Lakshmana returned. The jungle sank into an unnatural silence and Sita was afraid.

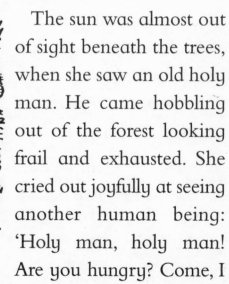

The sun was almost out of sight beneath the trees, when she saw an old holy man. He came hobbling out of the forest looking frail and exhausted. She cried out joyfully at seeing another human being: 'Holy man, holy man! Are you hungry? Come, I have some food to give you.'

'Yes, my dear, I am hungry. I have walked all day, and my bowl is empty.'

Sita ran inside the hut and scooped up some food on to a banana leaf. She rushed out again and, in her enthusiasm, almost stepped outside the circle. Just in time, as her toe touched the edge, she drew back. 'Holy man! Please come closer so that I can put this food into your bowl.'

The holy man stood rooted to the spot, his bowl still held out, just a few paces away but out of reach. His orange clothes seemed to burn like fire; his eyes glowed like coals. Yet, when  he spoke, his voice was so gentle, so kind. 'My dear, you know I am not allowed to go to you and take, you must come to me and give.'

'But . . . I promised not to step outside the circle . . .'

The holy man shrugged sadly. 'It is up to you.' He turned away.

Sita told herself, 'He is a holy man and he is old. It is against God's law to allow a holy man to depart empty handed. Surely I have nothing to fear from him? He is so close. All I have to do is leap out and, in just two steps, give him the food and get back inside the circle.' So she called again. 'Holy man, stay, I will come to you.'

The holy man paused and turned as Sita stepped outside the circle. She took one step, two, reached out, and put the food into the bowl.

Then something dreadful and terrifying and abominable happened. In one great flash of lightning, the gentle, sweet holy man grew and grew and grew, turning

16

into a monstrous, ten-headed, twenty-armed demon, with twenty rolling bloodshot eyes. It was Ravana, King of the Demons.

Like a whirlpool, Sita was sucked into Ravana's arms. From out of the sky, he summoned his chariot, pulled by two-headed demon horses, their hooves spraying sparks. With a wild laugh, he flung Sita inside. How she struggled and screamed as Ravana whipped up the horses and they galloped away into the sky to his island of Lanka.

Ravana begged Sita to marry him. The voices from his ten throats hummed sweetly like honey bees: 'Forget Rama,' they sang. 'Come and live with me and be my queen, and I will give you all that your heart desires.' He played the veena to her, hoping he could enchant her with his music and make her love him.

Day after day he came to her, but each time Sita had cried, 'Go away! I shall never marry you. Rama is my husband and he will be for ever.'

When at last Ravana realised that Sita would rather die than marry him, he flung her out of the palace and sent her to the wildest part of the garden to be taunted by his demons.

As Sita sat huddled under the banyan

tree, it seemed to her that even the stars looked unkind and the moon uncaring.

But something was moving across the heavens, swirling and bounding, sweeping through the Milky Way and plummeting towards earth. A falling star? A plunging comet? The brightness came closer, heading straight for her. Sita buried her face in her hands, blinded and terrified.

It was Hanuman, with Amrita wound into his tail. Like a shooting star, he descended. He landed without a sound, yet the earth trembled on his impact, and a deep anger rushed through him. Amrita felt his whole  body quake. 'What is it? What's wrong?' she stammered.

'Look at her! Look what they've done to the beautiful Princess Sita!' His whisper turned into a hiss of rage.

'Is that Princess Sita?' Amrita stared at the weeping young woman. 'Wife of our beloved Lord Rama?'

Amrita looked through the darkness at the dancing lights which she thought were fireflies. Then she realised they were the devilish eyes of demons, who whirled around Sita. They pulled her long hair, and pinched her arms till they were black and blue. They clawed at her with long curling fingernails, and bared their blackened teeth as if they would bite chunks out of her. And all the time they jeered and spat, 'SSSSSita! SSSSStupid girl! TTThhhhinks she's too good to MMMMMarry our king! Worse than a SSSSSnake!

LLLLower than a worm! We'll teach her. We'll teach her to know her place.'

Filled with pity and outrage, Amrita screamed, 'Stop it! Stop it at once! Leave her alone, you bunch of bullies,' and she rushed among the screeching, taunting demons and threw her arms round Sita to protect her.

In a flash, Hanuman turned himself into a tiny monkey and leapt into the tree. Coiling his tail round an over-hanging branch, he hung upside down until his mouth was close to Sita's ear, and he whispered sweetly, 'Take courage, dear Princess. Help is near. Rama is coming to rescue you. Be brave. It won't be long now.'

 Sita raised her head in wonder. She looked at Amrita and then at Hanuman.

'Rama? Is Rama near? Does he know I'm here?'

'He will soon.'

'Grrrr . . .' screamed a demon. It leapt in with a pointy, poky finger and jabbed Sita. She winced with pain.

Amrita lashed out. 'Get away! Get away you horrible creature.'

Hanuman's anger rushed through him. It was so great, it made him grow and grow and grow. He grew bigger than the tree. He grew bigger than ten trees standing end to end. He was so angry, the moon and stars disappeared and the night sky became even darker.

'How dare you treat the Princess Sita like that,' he thundered and, in his temper, he ripped up trees by their roots and hurled them among the demons; he scooped up hundreds of squealing monsters and flung them aside; he rushed about like a tornado, stamping and trampling as many of them as he could.

'Oh no, Hanuman! Stop, stop!' moaned Sita. 'Calm yourself. You cannot destroy the demons.'

Amrita saw this was true, for no matter how many demons Hanuman killed, thousands more rushed out. They swarmed all over him, and even though he was taller than a giant, they brought him crashing down.

'Hanuman!' Amrita whimpered with

fear, as they dragged him away. 'What will they do to him?' she asked, turning to Sita. But Sita had fainted.

All through that night, Amrita and Sita heard the chanting: 'Kill, kill, kill! Kill, kill, kill!'

The demons had dragged Hanuman before Ravana, King of the Demons.

'What shall we do with him?' they shrieked. 'Shall we chop him up into little pieces?'

But Lord Ravana shook his ten heads and smiled ten evil, cunning smiles. His ten voices crooned like a flock of doves.

 'No, no, no, no, no, no, no, no, no, no! Killing is too good for him. First we shall shame Hanuman – bring him down a peg. Then we shall use this snivelling, scrawny monkey

as our messenger. Ha! What better way of showing Rama that his powers are piffle in the wind compared to mine, and that he can do nothing to get back Sita?'

'Yesssss, yessss, yessss!' hissed the demons gleefully. 'But how shall we shame Hanuman?'

'What does Hanuman have that he treasures more than anything else?' demanded the King of the Demons.

The demons thought.

'Is it his silvery fur?'

'Is it his mighty strength?'

'Is it his wind-like speed?'

'No, no, no, no, no, no, no, no, no, NO!' roared Ravana.

'What then?' they asked running out of ideas.

'It is his TAIL, of course!' he bellowed. 'His tail, you idiots! Go get a fiery brand!'

Quick as a flash, several demons raced

off and returned with a huge burning brand. The flames soared from it, brighter than the sun. The demons recoiled from the terrible heat and hid their eyes.

'Hanuman! I could kill you, but I won't. Let's see what kind of a monkey you are without a tail!'

The demons fell about, howling with laughter as Ravana took the brand and held it to Hanuman's long, shining tail.

There was the sound of sizzling and crackling and spitting. Hanuman's tail began to burn. Then a sheet of fire flared into the sky as the tip of Hanuman's tail burst into flames.

Amrita watched in horror. 'Why did you start a fight, Hanuman?' she wept. 'Why didn't you just go and get Rama?' She held Sita fearfully in her arms.

'Hee, hee, hee!' Amrita couldn't believe her ears. Hanuman was chuckling. He

stood there with his tail on fire, laughing his head off while he became smaller and smaller and smaller. The demons tried to grab on to him, but only burnt their fingers or grasped at empty air. In a thrice, Hanuman had grown so small, they could see nothing except the glimmering fire of his tail. Like a glow worm, he slipped away.

Hanuman fled across the walls of the garden and on to the palace roofs, his tail burning like a meteor. But as he fled, he grew bigger again. He leapt from wall to wall and house to house setting the

 whole city alight from end to end.

Long into the night, Amrita heard the demons screaming and scattering in panic, not knowing whether to save their city or themselves.

'Thank goodness,' Sita murmured with relief.

'He's got away.' The princess leant her head against Amrita's shoulder and slept for the very first time since Ravana had tricked her in the jungle.

I hope when Sita is rescued, I'll be rescued too, thought Amrita sinking into sleep herself.

3 Amrita's new clothes

'Wake up, wake up, child!' Amrita's granny was shaking her. 'Naughty girl! Look at the mess! Fancy eating monkey-nuts in bed. Get up now. You'll have to clean your room before we go shopping to buy you Diwali clothes.'

Amrita got the dustpan and brush and swept up the shells. As she did, she sang, 'It's true. It all really happened. But surely it's not over yet?' Then she remembered Sita, and sat back on her heels. 'How come I'm home? Poor Sita! She's all alone with those demons. I should have stayed until Rama came. Hanuman, where are you?'

She ran to the window wondering if she would catch a glimpse of the Monkey God – up the apple tree, on the fence, behind the dustbin, down the alleyway. She saw a gleam of fur and a tip of tail, but it was only next door's cat.

'Come on, come on, come on!' her mother's voice urged her from downstairs. 'Granny's waiting for you. She wants to get going. Everyone will be out shopping today. Diwali is almost upon us – and I still have so much cooking to do for the party tomorrow.'

'Oh dear!' sighed Amrita. 'Everyone's

going to be moody today.' She followed her grandmother out of the gate.

'Don't frown, child,' snapped Granny, 'otherwise you'll have grumpy wrinkles when you're old.' A deep furrow divided her eyebrows as she wagged her finger at Amrita. Then, hugging her shopping bag close to her body, Granny stumped off towards the town centre.

Amrita would usually have been hopping and skipping ahead, and her granny would have been calling out, 'Don't go so fast, child! Have pity on your poor old granny.' But, today, Amrita was trailing behind listlessly, and Granny was grumbling, 'Keep up, keep up! What's wrong with you, child?'

'Ow!' exclaimed Amrita,

as she felt her ponytail tugged hard. 'Stop it!' She whirled round expecting it to be Steven, the boy from a few doors along, who was always so annoying. But there was no one there.

A tickly puff of wind blew into one ear  then into the other, making her squeal with laughter. But in the next breath she was shouting, 'Ow! That hurt!' as something trod on her toe. She hopped about. 'Ow! That hurt!' mimicked a whispery voice.

Then something tripped her up. 'Ow, ow, ow!' yelped Amrita. 'What are you doing? Stop it!'

'Stop it, stop it, stop it!' mimicked the voice sounding like Granny.

'That's no way to talk to your grandmother,' Granny stopped and turned round with a scowl. 'Are you making fun of me?' she asked suspiciously.

'I wasn't talking to you, Granny,' Amrita tried to explain.

'To whom then, may I ask? I see no one else. Do you make a habit of talking to trees or lampposts?'

'Oh, Granny, I thought . . .'

'And why are you dawdling behind like this?' continued Granny without taking a breath. 'Don't you want a new Diwali dress?'

'Oh yes! I do!' Amrita tried to sound pleased, but she knew what kind of dress her grandmother would insist on buying her, and she felt ridiculous already. It would be the kind of dress she hated – shocking-pink and all frills, bobs and bows, and fancy stitching and smocking, and lace and layers of petticoats, which stuck out as if she was wearing an umbrella. She would have to wear matching pink socks and matching ribbons in her hair – and she'd look an idiot. Amrita sighed, then gave a wriggly scream as something which felt like a beetle dropped down the back of her T-shirt.

'Really, Amrita,' snapped Granny impatiently. 'Walk in front where I can see you. And stop all this nonsense!' She gazed with exasperation at her grand-daughter leaping about, tearing at her clothes.

'Something's gone down my back. I'm sure it's a creepy-crawly!' Amrita bellowed. 'Get it out, get it out!'

Granny held her still and lifted up her T-shirt. 'Ha!' she snorted. 'That's what comes of eating peanuts in bed! You even

got them in your clothes.'
She held out the husk of an
empty shell.

'Tch, tch, tch!' a tongue
clicked reprovingly near
Amrita's ear.

Amrita swung round.
'Hanuman?' she whispered.
'Are you here?'

'Am I here? Am I there? Am I anywhere?'

She felt the breath of his voice tickling
her cheek and the back of her neck.

'You cheeky monkey!' she chortled. 'It
was you playing tricks on me.' She heard
a rustle of leaves above her head and the
sound of scampering. She caught a
glimpse of tail and a twitch of ears in a
cherry tree along the road. 'Are we
going to rescue Sita?'

'Buy your dress first!' ordered

Hanuman's voice in her ear. 'You have to look right for the occasion.'

'Oh, but I'll never look right in what Granny will buy me. How I hate dresses.'

'Wear a salvar kameez. That is much more suitable,' suggested Hanuman.

'She'll never let me. Granny just loves frilly dresses.'

'Hmm! We'll see about that!' muttered Hanuman.

They reached the High Street. After gazing into the windows of several saree and dress shops, Granny steered Amrita into Rita's Sweeter Maid which specialised in clothes for girls.

At Granny's request, Rita brought out all her frilliest dresses, and Amrita had to try on one after the other. Each time, she came out of the cubicle and stood in front of the mirror to be judged by her grandmother. In the reflection, she glimpsed a swish of tail disappearing among the racks of clothes and long black fingers whisking through the hangers. She caught beady black eyes peering at her between the hanging garments.

'This one?' Amrita asked Hanuman silently.

'Terrible!' His face screwed up with disgust time after time, because, as soon as Amrita stood in front of the long mirror, the dress she wore looked like rags.

Even when Amrita put on the bright pink dress, stiff as newly spun candy floss on a stick, with layers of net petticoat, and bright sequins which sparkled

on the bodice, and large floppy bows which bounced on each sleeve, Granny looked puzzled. 'I don't understand it. You look like a rag-doll. It looked so nice on the hanger ... Rita is losing her touch, I tell you. What to do?'

Then Hanuman, who had been hiding behind a whole rack of clothes, held up a beautiful salvar kameez and shook it at Amrita. 'This one, this one!' he whispered. It was cotton and silk and softly yellow like a ripening mango; it had delicate embroidery round the neck and sleeves like the twining tracery of laced marble; the dupatta was light and flowing, pouring over her arms like water as she took it from him.

'May I try this, Granny?' she asked.

'Well ...' Granny liked the bright pink, frilly dress, but surprised even herself by changing her mind. 'You can try it, dear – but ... go, go, go, be quick about it. We can't hang about all day.'

When Amrita appeared from the changing-room, Granny couldn't say a word, and Rita was flabbergasted. 'Goodness me! I didn't even know I had such a salvar kameez. How could I forget? It fits as though it were made for you. She's got to have this outfit, I tell you.'

Granny nodded and finally spoke in a hushed voice, 'Yes, you're right. It makes her look quite pretty. Yes, yes, child. That's the one for Diwali.'

The new salvar kameez hung from the hanger on the back of Amrita's bedroom door. She could see it from her bed.

39

Moonbeams fell upon it, threading themselves in and out of the pale yellow material so that it glistened.

'It's time to put it on.' Hanuman's voice filled the room like an aroma of honeysuckle and evening air. Amrita obeyed. When she was dressed and had combed out her hair, she stood in the window and stared down at the dark garden. Hanuman came bounding out of the starry sky, his tail trailing like a comet and, this time, Amrita leapt fearlessly on to his back.

4 The final conflict

Ravana ground his teeth. In every
corner of India, in all the cities, towns
and villages, in the lonely expanses of
the desert, along the shores of the ocean,
up in the chilly peaks of the Himalayas,
people were building models of him.
They were tall, evil-looking likenesses
with ten heads, red glaring eyes, tongues
dripping with blood and twenty arms
which flayed in all directions.

When they finished building the
models, they stuck them up on a high
platform and carried them through the

streets to the banks of a river, where they burnt them and cast the ashes into the water.

'Huh!' sneered Ravana. 'Think they can get rid of me, do they? Don't they realise nobody can kill me?'

Ravana took up his veena and began to play, his many fingers strumming the strings. No one played like him. His sounds enchanted all who listened.

Ravana was sad. He knew that many would obey him, many would flatter him, many would fear him. But no one would love him. He longed for Sita's love. Her beauty and goodness flowed like honey. But she was Rama's wife and she loved her husband.

Rama. The name filled Ravana with

fury. He strode to the ramparts of his palace and looked out across the ocean to the dark shores of the mainland. He knew that Rama was gathering an army to come and fight him and rescue Sita. An army of monkeys and bears with long sharp nails and ripping teeth. He looked at the heaving ocean and smiled; that was his greatest protection. Monkeys can't swim; bears can't fly. How would they cross the sea? He was safe.

Ravana stretched out his twenty arms. He stretched and stretched until he became as broad as the night, and all his twenty eyes became just one all-seeing eye. Then, in a vast quilt of darkness and plucking strings, he rolled himself over the surface of the earth.

Amrita had heard the wonderful music, and she and Hanuman danced among the stars.

'Where does the music come from?' she asked breathlessly.

'It is Ravana,' answered Hanuman. 'He was given the gift of music before he became bad, when he was loved by the Creator, Lord Vishnu. Now, it is the only good thing he has left, and he plays to remember what he once was.'

When they crossed the Himalayas, Hanuman carried Amrita southwards over the darkening land. At the far edge of the ocean, where the sea sparkled in the setting sun, Amrita saw that the

shore was swarming with monkeys. They seemed to be building a bridge.

Hanuman crossed the ocean and landed on the island of Lanka. He made himself and Amrita invisible so they could search for Sita.

A hush hung over the demon city but, lined on the ramparts of the palace, the demon warriors sharpened their weapons and waited.

Hanuman and Amrita couldn't find Sita. She was no longer in the garden. They went into every chamber in the palace, from the highest terraces, down to the cellars in the bowels of the earth. At last, they found her in the deepest, darkest dungeon. The light from Hanuman's eyes cast a soft glow. Sita crouched in a corner, her face on her knees.

'Ah, Princess!' he sighed and bowed respectfully. 'We have found you. Be brave. It won't be long now before you are rescued.'

Sita's pale face gleamed sadly in the darkness.

'I want you to stay here with Sita,' said Hanuman to Amrita.

For the first time, Amrita was afraid. 'Don't leave me,' she pleaded. 'It's so dark.'

'Sita needs you,' said the Monkey God. 'All over the world battles are about to begin. Light will win over Darkness; Good over Evil; Prince Rama over Ravana. Stay with Sita and give her courage, for the sound of battle will be terrifying.'

'Yes, yes, of course I will stay,' whispered Amrita. She knelt down by the Princess Sita. 'I'll stay with you until Rama comes.'

Sita smiled, then Hanuman was gone and they were plunged into pitch darkness.

The battle was terrible. All through the day and night and the next day, the ground shuddered beneath their feet. Sita and Amrita huddled in the darkness. They thought the universe was being destroyed.

Who was winning and who was losing? Could Rama kill Ravana? Every time he struck off one head, another grew in its place. But Rama finally took up his

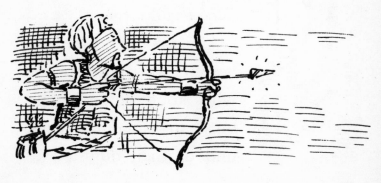

special golden arrow. He fitted it to his bow and aimed at Ravana's heart.

An almighty crash shook every stone in the city. Sita and Amrita thought the end of the world had come. The stillness was like the quiet after a storm, when the rain has stopped and the thunder has died away. What had happened? Would someone come to rescue them? Neither

dared speak.

Then, without warning, the great door burst open. A blinding shaft of daylight cut across the floor. A figure, tall as a giant filled the doorway.

Amrita's head stayed bowed, not daring to see who stood before them, but Sita raised her eyes, and as they adjusted to the brightness, she gave a cry of joy. 'Hanuman!'

Hanuman held out his hand to Sita. 'Ravana is dead! Come, Princess! Your husband, Prince Rama, is waiting for you.'

Rama and Sita were reunited and their fourteen years in the jungle were over. They could go home to the Kingdom of Ayodhya.

5 Diwali

Hanuman carried Amrita over the world. Below them, they saw people dressed in their new Diwali clothes, greeting each other on the streets; they saw the exchange of presents and sweets; they saw the young men lighting fireworks and the girls shrieking with delight. And as night began to fall, they saw the thousands upon thousands of little saucers of wicks and oil being placed along verandas and steps, window ledges and balconies, to light the way for Rama and Sita on their long journey back home.

'It's time for you to go back too, Amrita,' said Hanuman softly. 'It is Diwali, the Festival of Light and the New Year. You must be ready for the Goddess Lakshmi to come into your home.'

Below them, the grey towns and cities still slept. Thousands of homes had been scrubbed clean. Hedges had been cut and paths swept. And in front of thousands of homes there were rangoli patterns made from sprinkled rice flour and coloured spice powders. As they came closer to Amrita's house, they saw that her mother and aunt had created a

beautiful pattern outside the front door and, edging the paths and lawns and all the windowsills, were rows of saucers of oil waiting to be lit.

'Yes!' murmured Hanuman approvingly. 'Your household is ready for Diwali. Lakshmi can come here.'

Amrita slid back into her bedroom, then turned to Hanuman hovering in space outside her window. He was shining, silver – the Monkey God. She wanted to speak, but had no words, so she clasped her hands in reverence and thanks.

Hanuman smiled and raised a hand in farewell, then he too, pressed his palms together in a namaste – and was gone.

The next day Amrita helped her

mother and grandmother as they prepared for the big Diwali party they were holding at their house that evening. Wonderful smells of cooking wafted through the house; platters of bhaji and pakoras, kofti and spiced sausages were carried through. Naan bread and poories, rice and lentils, spiced vegetables and salad creations soon crowded the party table.

Darkness fell. The excitement grew. Grandmother and mother went out with long, burning tapers, and lit the little oil-lamps. Amrita put on her special Diwali salvar kameez. The guests began to arrive – gleaming as though they were new-born; fresh as if they had sprung into creation in their glittering new clothes.

As the party got going, chatter and laughter mixing in with music and singing, Amrita crept silently upstairs. Suddenly, she wanted to be alone, and to remember everything that had happened with Hanuman.

The party ended, the guests went home and the house became still, as sleep overcame everyone. Outside, the oil-lamps still glimmered. Amrita stared out into the black night. The darkness extended into eternity. Her eye fixed upon a strange creamy light. It grew brighter and brighter and brighter. It increased with an energy which seemed to come from all the gods put together: from Agni, the God of Fire, Varun, the God of Water; it came from Brahma, Shiva and Vishnu; from the mountains and the oceans and from all creation. The light was swirling like churned milk. Out of the churning rose Lakshmi, floating on a golden lotus flower. She looked like Sita; she was Sita. Sita was Lakshmi, the great Goddess of Wealth and Prosperity. Energy flowed from her feet, arms, waist, thighs, nose, teeth, eyes and throat. She paused for a moment over the rangoli pattern at the threshold as if to admire it – then swept inside. Her light filled the house and, for a moment, it seemed as though Amrita's house was the very centre of the universe. Then Lakshmi was gone, gently rippling away into the night, and all that was left was the scent of flowers.

When Amrita woke the next morning, there was a scattering of monkey-nut shells and blossom across her carpet. She knew that every year the battle between Good and Evil would be fought out again and again, so long as the world existed. But for one of those battles, Amrita had been there.

As she stood before the mirror and brushed out her hair, she heard a faint clapping. A monkey-nut flew through the air and struck her on the shoulder. Amrita laughed out loud, 'I know you're there, Hanuman!' She ran to the window. The bough of the apple tree was swaying. She glimpsed a long silver tail. It swished and twitched and then was still.

Glossary

Agni	God of Fire
bhaji	vegetable doughnut
Brahma	God of Creation
Diwali	Festival of Light
dupatta	veil, part of Indian dress
Hanuman	the Monkey God
Himalayas	mountain range in central Asia
Kali	Goddess of Destruction
kofti	meatball
Lakshmi/Sita	Goddess of Wealth and Prosperity
naan	type of bread
namaste	greeting
Narakasura	God of Darkness
pakoras	type of savoury
poories	type of bread
Rama	Vishnu on earth
rangoli	pattern

Ravana	God of Demons
saree	Indian dress
salvar kameez	Indian tunic and pyjamas
Sita	Lakshmana on earth
Varun	God of Water
Vayu	God of Wind
veena	stringed musical instrument
Vishnu	Preserver of Creation